THE
LAST
BROTHER

A CIVIL WAR TALE

TRINKA HAKES NOBLE ~ ILLUSTRATED BY ROBERT PAPP

For my brother Danny–
With love,

–T.H.N.

Dedicated to those who love our country.

–R.P.

Sleeping Bear Press wishes to acknowledge
Sue Boardman, Licensed Battlefield Guide,
for reading and reviewing the manuscript.

Robert Papp wishes to thank his friend Danny and also
the McClellan Rangers Reenactment Association, for
providing assistance in his research for *The Last Brother*.

Text Copyright © 2006 Trinka Hakes Noble
Illustration Copyright © 2006 Robert Papp

Sleeping Bear Press

310 North Main Street, Suite 300
Chelsea, MI 48118
www.sleepingbearpress.com

THOMSON
GALE

© 2006 Thomson Gale, a part of the Thomson Corporation.

Thomson, Star Logo and Sleeping Bear Press are trademarks
and Gale is a registered trademark used herein under license.

Printed and bound in China

10 9 8 7 6 5 4 3 2 1

Library of Congress Cataloging-in-Publication Data

Noble, Trinka Hakes.
The last brother : a Civil War tale / written by Trinka Hakes Noble
; illustrated by Robert Papp.p. cm.
Summary: Eleven-year-old Gabe enlists in the Union Army in
Pennsylvania along with his older brother Davy and, as a bugler,
does his best to protect Davy during the Battle of Gettysburg.
ISBN 1-58536-253-0
1. Gettysburg, Battle of, Gettysburg, Pa., 1863–Juvenile
fiction. [1. Gettysburg, Battle of, Gettysburg, Pa., 1863–Fiction
2. Brothers–Fiction. 3. Bugle–Fiction. 4. United States–History–
Civil War, 1861-1865–Fiction.] I. Papp, Robert, ill.
II. Title.
PZ7.N6715La 2006
[Fic]–dc22   2005029529

AUTHOR'S NOTE

The Civil War is sometimes called the boys' war because those who served were so young. Many drummers and buglers were between the ages of ten and fourteen. The inspiration for *The Last Brother* came from my own family history. Nearly one hundred of my ancestors were in the Civil War, which they called the States War. One large Hakes farming family from upstate New York sent all their sons. The youngest, a fourteen-year-old drummer, was the only one who returned. This tragic loss was not uncommon on both sides.

But it wasn't until I walked the battlefield at Gettysburg that I began to realize the depth and enormity of what happened there. The culmination of this three-day battle at Pickett's Charge seemed beyond reason, yet soldiers did survive in pockets up and down the three-mile-long battle line. The highly emotional content of this story was drawn from that experience.

The Last Brother was written with deep respect and honor, not only for my ancestors, but for all who served in the Civil War.

–Trinka Hakes Noble

On the morning of July 1st, 1863, the peaceful little town of Gettysburg awoke, early as usual. Front porches were swept clean, feather beds aired, and blackberry jam bubbled on the stove. In the town square, old men dozed in the shade while small barefoot boys scampered toward Seminary Ridge carrying fishing poles and berry pails.

One mile across from Seminary Ridge rose Cemetery Ridge flanked by Little Round Top and Big Round Top to the south and Cemetery and Culp's Hill to the north. In the rich valley below, tidy farms and fields spread out like a patchwork quilt stitched together with split rail fences.

Yet the Civil War had raged for two years. Gettysburg was only seven miles from the Mason-Dixon Line. When rumors reached the old men that Confederate troops had pushed north into Pennsylvania, they kept a watchful lookout for signs of war. But the barefoot boys up on Seminary Ridge saw it first...two massive clouds of dust gathering on either horizon as two armies moved closer.

In one cloud of dust marched a young boy in a blue uniform, with a full knapsack, a canteen, and a brass bugle slung over his shoulder. His name was Gabriel and he was a bugler in the Union Army, even though he was only eleven.

Gabe was the youngest in a big Pennsylvania farm family of four boys and five girls. He'd run away with his brother Davy, who was sixteen, to join up. When the recruiting officer asked Davy his age, Davy honestly replied, "I'm over eighteen" because he had slipped a piece of paper inside his shoe with 18 penciled on it.

Then he pointed at Gabe. "Think you can blow a bugle for the Keystone State, boy?"

Gabriel nodded, "I can learn, sir."

Lots of boys Davy's age got the war fever, hankering for adventure and glory. But Gabe had his own reason for tagging after Davy.

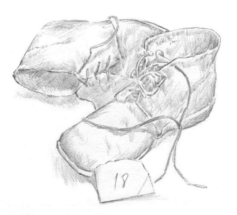

Joshua and Tucker, Gabe's two oldest brothers, had marched off to join the Union Army when President Lincoln first called for volunteers after the firing on Fort Sumter in 1861.

"It's just for 90 days," Josh and Tuck assured their Ma and Pa. "Come harvesttime, we'll be back. Can't expect these two little runts to handle it," they joked, playfully cuffing Davy and Gabe.

But Ma and Pa looked serious. "You are the sons of old Pennsylvania now," they said.

How proudly Josh and Tuck marched off in their blue uniforms. Davy and Gabe had raced alongside, shouting "the Union forever!" while their sisters cheered, waving white handkerchiefs.

But harvesttime came and went. Ninety days stretched into a year, then two, until finally, one day, the sad news came and those ninety days had become forever. That's when Gabe knew Davy would enlist and he would follow.

So now Gabe and Davy were the boys in blue. Gabe pulled his cap low and squinted. He searched for Davy marching with the 71st Pennsylvania, but the dust was too thick. So many regiments and brigades had joined the long blue column, with flags flying from every northern state from Maine to Michigan to Minnesota. Gabe had never seen so many soldiers.

"Keep up, boy!" ordered a sergeant. "No stragglers! We got a full day's march to Gettysburg."

"Yes, sir," Gabe obeyed and quickstepped forward, keeping his eye on Lancer up ahead, the major's powerful chestnut charger.

Lancer was a trained military horse, with the letters U.S. branded on his hindquarter. Neither busting shells nor flying bullets spooked him. He'd charge into battle, knowing all the commands almost before they were called.

Like Lancer, Gabe knew all the commands, too. There were over 60 different battle calls for young buglers to learn. The problem in the Civil War was that the Confederate Army had the same calls. So it was crucial for troops to learn the style of their own bugler, especially in battle. So Gabriel practiced long and hard. And to make sure his regiment knew it was him, he put a little uplifting lilt in each one. But unlike Lancer, Gabe had never been in a real battle.

The next day they made camp below Cemetery Ridge. Already fighting and skirmishes had broken out. Cannon smoke hung heavy in the air. Up on Cemetery Hill Gabe could see dozens of artillery batteries pointed toward the enemy.

Immediately, the major called for scouts and Davy was the first to step forward. Gabe nervously watched his brother vanish into the smoke while Army mules rumbled by hauling more cannons and heavy caissons loaded with grapeshot and canister shells.

Gabe knew he wouldn't be needed right away, so he slipped into the densely wooded hillsides and sat by a stream to practice battle calls. He stuffed his handkerchief in his bugle's bell and softly blew "commence fire." To his surprise, a bugle softly answered from across the stream with "cease fire." Gabe looked but saw no one, so he blew "fix bayonets" and instantly heard "unfix bayonets." Astounded, Gabe stood and blew a full "charge" and back came "retreat"!

Suddenly a boy peeked out from the bushes with a bugle in one hand, a fishing pole in the other, and a big old grin on his dirty freckled face. He splashed across the stream to Gabe.

"Howdy! I'm Orlee. You sure know how to blow that horn."

"I'm Gabriel," Gabe smiled, happy to meet a boy his own age.

Orlee started gabbing like they were old friends. "Gabriel … now that's a right fancy name. My Paw wanted to give me a fancy name but Maw wanted to call me Lee. Paw kept thinkin' up fancier and fancier names like Beauregard and Bertram, but Maw kept saying 'or Lee.' She had to say it so many times that pretty soon they just called me Orlee."

Gabe laughed and Orlee chuckled. It'd been a long time since either boy had laughed.

"Bet'cha thought I was named after General Robert E. Lee, didn't ya?" Orlee winked. "Nah, not in the Mississippi hills I growed up in. Maw figured a name like Lee with just three letters, 'specially with two of them the same, would be real easy for a feller to keep track of. A right smart woman, my Maw."

Then Orlee paused and quietly asked, "Do your home folks call you Gabe?"

Gabe nodded silently and for a moment both boys tried to remember the sound of their mothers' voices. That's when Gabe noticed Orlee had scratched his name and regiment, the 11th Mississippi, on the bell of his bugle, just in case.

But Orlee wasn't silent for long. "I was sneakin' in a little fishin'," he teased, "and you come by and blew 'commence fire' and those fish skedaddled faster than fat hens on market day!"

"Bet they're hiding right under that fallen log," Gabe grinned, remembering the best place to catch brook trout back home was under the covered bridge.

So the two boys sat down to fish. Soon Orlee asked, "Got anything to trade?" Gabe swapped some army hardtack for a bit of Orlee's fatback. Then Orlee handed Gabe some Virginia pipe tobacco and said, "Don't smoke it. It's like gold. You can trade tobacco for anything." So Gabe gave Orlee his ration of coffee and they divided the fish.

As they departed, the two young buglers played taps to each other as a way of saying farewell. Gabe couldn't help but notice a sad downturn in his friend's bugle call and it worried him.

But, for a short time, the old hills of Pennsylvania shielded the northern boy and the southern lad from what was to come.

When Gabe got back to camp, Davy hadn't returned. But there were other duties for a bugle boy to perform. So Gabe carried firewood, filled canteens, and watered the major's horse.

While Lancer drank, Gabe leaned into his side and lightly traced a long, jagged scar across the horse's broad chest. "Lancer," he whispered, "I wish you could tell me what it's like to be in battle."

When Gabe thought about Josh and Tuck, he wanted to cry. Now Davy was in the fight. What if Davy didn't come back like Josh and Tuck? For a moment, Gabe buried his face in Lancer's mane as the great horse gently wrapped his powerful neck and head around the boy.

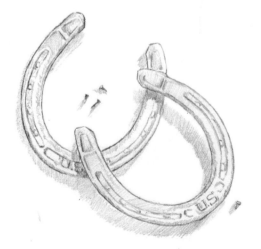

Suddenly, Lancer whinnied low. Gabe jerked around. There stood Orlee, solemn, in full uniform, his finger pressed against his lips.

"Gabe," he whispered seriously. "We got battle orders. My whole regiment's assembled just yonder." Then he silently waved the back of his hand at Gabe. "Best hightail it out of here with that horse before they see you."

Gabe grabbed Lancer's reins, shot a nervous glance toward the clearing, and silently mouthed the words "thank you" as he pulled Lancer around.

"Gabe," Orlee softly called after him,
"if you ever git to Mississippi someday…"

Gabe nodded over his shoulder, "God willing,
we'll fish again if…" but Orlee had already
vanished. Gabe hurried Lancer out of sight.

It was long after dark before Davy returned, exhausted, his face streaked with gunpowder and sweat. He wolfed down the fish stew Gabe had saved for him, drained a fresh canteen, and sprawled on the ground until he caught his breath.

"We fought the Rebs in the woods today," he said hoarsely, his eyes closed. "Gabe, some of them aren't any older than me." Gabe nodded, but didn't tell Davy about Orlee.

"The Confederates are all over that far ridge, down near Little Round Top, too," Davy reported. "They captured the town. Got sharpshooters in the church towers. Folks are hiding in their cellars. Almost took Culp's Hill. Gabe, we're nearly out-flanked. See those campfires along Cemetery Ridge? Well, some of them are fake, kept going by a couple picket guards, trying to fool the Confederates into thinking we've got more men."

Davy stood, anxious to clean and reload his rifle, then paused. "Get some sleep, little brother. We'll see heavy action tomorrow." Gabe could see the burning embers reflected in Davy's eyes. "Gabe," he said slowly, "all the Pennsylvania boys volunteered to go first, so stay on the safe side of the major's horse tomorrow." Then he was gone.

All through the night the Union campfires burned on Cemetery Ridge, but Gabe couldn't sleep. He kept thinking about Davy and Orlee, afraid of what might happen tomorrow. When he peeked from his bedroll, the flickering firelight cast ominous shadows of troops digging defensive earthworks, mules hauling heavy supply wagons, and reinforcements creeping in under the cover of darkness.

At dawn, the campfires blinked out, one by one. When Gabe sounded reveille for his regiment, scores of other regimental buglers echoed up and down the ridge. There, concealed just below Cemetery Ridge, was the whole Union Army—entrenched, ready and waiting.

That morning Gabe's regiment could hear heavy gunfire as they marched into position on the north section of Cemetery Ridge behind the gunners. Gabe stood next to Lancer, at his post, bugle in hand. Davy waited in the front line, his rifle loaded, at the ready.

Then, at midday, from across the valley, Confederate cannons opened fire and Union cannons roared back with a thundering blast that shook the earth. Shells exploded everywhere. The deafening blast knocked Gabe off balance. He grabbed onto Lancer.

"Hold steady, boys," shouted the major. "They can't dislodge the Old Keystone!"

The Union artillery gunners were relentless, firing volley after volley. Gunpowder smoke burned Gabe's eyes, choked his throat, and scorched his lungs. The Confederate cannons stubbornly pounded back, ripping into the Union lines. With each blast, blinding dirt, sizzling shell fragments, and lead grapeshot hissed helter-skelter through the ranks. The massive bombardment kept up, nonstop, from both sides for two deadly hours. But the Keystone held.

When the suffocating smoke cleared, Gabe stiffened with fear at what he saw. For there, pouring out from behind the trees on Seminary Ridge, were thousands upon thousands of Confederate troops, advancing across the valley. What had once been a patchwork quilt of tidy farms and fields was now a swarming mass of soldiers in gray, charging toward the Union lines. Chills shot up Gabe's spine. Lancer's head jerked violently, his ears flattened.

"FORWARD!" ordered the major as the first bullets whizzed overhead. Somehow Gabe blew "forward" and the 71st Infantry moved in front of the field guns and cannons like a precision machine and took cover behind a stone wall.

"Ready on the firing line! COMMENCE FIRE!" Gabe could barely breathe but sounded the command and a storm of bullets smashed into the Confederate lines.

"FIRE AT WILL! FIRE AT WILL! FIRE AT WILL!" was shouted up and down the Union lines. Gabe shook, yet stayed on his feet. Blood streamed down Lancer's leg. Davy blurred into a solid fortress of blue, firing and reloading, firing and reloading, firing and reloading. But still the Confederates kept coming, firing back, determined to break the Union lines. The gunfire from both sides was so intense, so thick, that some Union and Confederate bullets actually collided in midair and fell to the ground. But many hit their mark, until both sides had nearly exhausted their ammo.

Then, the major drew his sword, pointed it skyward and yelled "**FOR PENNSYLVANIA AND THE UNION–CHARGE!!**"

Lancer lunged forward…but Gabe hesitated.

For an instant, Gabe wanted to sound "retreat," to save Davy fighting in the front lines. But there was Orlee, somewhere on the other side. Again, the major commanded "**CHARGE! CHARGE!!**" but no sound came from the boy. What could he do?

Suddenly, Gabe knew what to do. He forced a deep gulp of air and blew "charge" as fast as he could. Then, unnoticed in the confusion of battle, he ran onto the battlefield and instantly blew "retreat," mimicking Orlee's style. And for a brief moment, the firing stopped.

In this deadliest of battles, later known as Pickett's Charge, with thousands of casualties in just fifty minutes, there was only one small section of the battle line where not a single life was lost on either side.

At dusk on that final day of the bloodiest battle in American history, a young bugler climbed to the top of Cemetery Hill. He stood on a caisson to make himself taller, for he was only eleven. He faced west across the valley, raised his bugle to his lips, and played taps.

The bittersweet refrain seemed to rise up from the boy's very soul and join in harmony with the softening twilight. Both gray and blue caps were removed and held over hearts. The shell-shocked folks of Gettysburg emerged from their cellars and, for a moment, the pain of the wounded was eased. And, far out on the battle-field, one injured horse rose to his feet and slowly limped toward the sound.

The boy held the last note for a very long time, so long that it seemed to reach eternity.

Then, faintly, from far across the valley, a bugler answered with a sad downturn that echoed through the darkening hills. The boy in blue drew to attention, lowered his bugle, and saluted. The Battle of Gettysburg was over.

All through that long night, the young bugler tenderly cared for his wounded brother and the injured horse. And when the first pale pink blush of dawn crept into the eastern sky, he sat by the campfire next to his brother and etched these words on his bugle …

For all my brothers, on this day and forever…

It was July 4, 1863.

T 40250

E
Noble

Noble, Trinka Hakes
The Last Brother

DATE DUE
